This book belongs to:

_____

_____

This edition published by Parragon Books Ltd in 2016 and distributed by

Parragon Inc.
440 Park Avenue South, 13th Floor
New York, NY 10016
www.parragon.com

Copyright © Parragon Books Ltd 2016
Text © Hollins University

Written by Margaret Wise Brown
Illustrated by Emma Levey
Edited by Becky Wilson and Michael Diggle
Designed by Anna Madin
Production by Juliet Fountain

ISBN 978-1-4748-4658-5
Printed in China

THE
little
BUNNIES

PaRragon

Bath • New York • Cologne • Melbourne • Delhi
Hong Kong • Shenzhen • Singapore

Come, look!
Close the book.

We are so many
That if you don't look ...

We'll jump in your hair
And tickle your ears—
Tweak your nose
And nip your toes,

We will hide
Behind rocks,
Behind bushes,
And up in trees.

So follow our happy

hops and springs

And we'll show you some little things.

Little things that play and sleep
In the grassblade forests deep,

In

the

wild

green

grass.

See! Little mice that squeak in twos ...

And little frogs

that like to snooze

in hammocks made of leaves.

Look! Little butterflies in the air,
That flitter here and flutter there ...

And disappear
as quick as a wink,

When noses twitch
and big eyes blink

in wonder at their wings.

Sometimes we sing them a little song,
Soft as a wind that doesn't last long—

Sometimes to the wrong tune,
Hushed by whispering trees.

We sing a song of little things,

Of little bugs and flies with wings ...

Of flakes of snow

and drops of rain

And little flowers on the plain ...

Of stars and moons

and carrot cake ...

Of little bunnies wide awake,
Laughing till their tummies ache.

And little dreams that come with sleep,

Of the grassblade forests
deep in the wild green grass.